THIS BLOOMSBURY BOOK

BELONGS TO

....

For Elsie and Emile – M.R.

For Rebecca – A.R.

First published in Great Britain in 2007 by Bloomsbury Publishing Plc
36 Soho Square, London, W1D 3QY

This paperback and audio CD edition first published in 2008

Audio CD produced by Jeff Capel at The Audio Workshop
Read by Michael Rosen

A CIP catalogue record of this book is available from the British Library

ISBN 978 0 7475 7786 7

Printed and bound in China

3 5 7 9 10 8 6 4 2

All papers used by Bloomsbury Publishing Plc are natural, recyclable
products made from wood grown in well-managed forests. The manufacturing
processes conform to the environmental regulations of the country of origin.

The Bear in the Cave

By Michael Rosen   Illustrated by Adrian Reynolds

BLOOMSBURY
CHILDREN'S
BOOKS

I'm a bear in a cave.
In a cave?
In a cave.
All alone.

I'm a bear all alone.
All alone?
All alone.

And I sing to myself all day.
Do bee doo
Do bee doo
Do bee doodily doo.

I walk by the sea.
By the sea?
By the sea.

And I play with the waves all day.
Splishety splash
Splishety splash
Splishety splashety splish.

One day I heard a noise.
Heard a noise?
Heard a noise.

It came from far away.
Far away?
Far away.

The sound of the city in my ears.
Vroomy vroom
Vroomy vroom
Vroomy vroomity vroom.

So I got a ticket to the city.
To the city?
To the city.

And I travelled to the city far away.
Chuffity chuff
Chuffity chuff
Chuff chuffity chuff.

I saw buildings up to the sky.
Up to the sky?
Up to the sky.

I saw people rushing past.
Rushing past?
Rushing past.

And cars flew by all day.
Whooshy whoosh
Whooshy whoosh
Whooshy whooshity whoosh.

I went to the market.
To the market?
To the market.

Bananas, fish and shoes.
Fish and shoes?
Fish and shoes.

With people shouting out all day.
You gotta buy that
You gotta buy this
You gotta buy thissety that.

I ran to the park.
To the park?
To the park.

I sat on a swing.
On a swing?
On a swing.

But everyone laughed at me there.
Hee hee hee
Hee hee hee
Hee hee heedily hee.

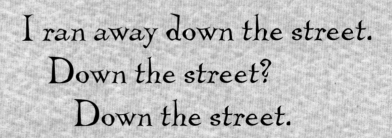

I ran away down the street.
Down the street?
Down the street.

I sat on a bench.
On a bench?
On a bench.

And I heard some people coming near.
They said, 'It's a bear!'
It's a bear?
It's a bear.

'It looks like it's lost.'
Like it's lost?
Like it's lost.

'Let's take it home by the sea.
Follow us
Follow us
Follow ussity us.'

Through the park.
Hee hee hee
Hee hee hee
Hee hee heedily hee.

Through the market.
You gotta buy this
You gotta buy that
You gotta buy thissety this.

Past the cars.
Whooshy whoosh
Whooshy whoosh
Whooshy whooshity whoosh.

On the train.
   Chuffity chuff
    Chuffity chuff
     Chuff chuffity chuff.

The city in my ears.
   Vroomy vroom
    Vroomy vroom
     Vroomy vroomity vroom.

To play by the waves.
Splishety splash
Splishety splash
Splishety splashety splish.

To sing all day.

Do bee doo, do bee doo,

do bee doodily . . . shh.

Enjoy more fantastic books by Michael Rosen
The Children's Laureate

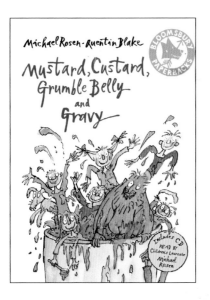

Mustard, Custard, Grumble Belly and Gravy

by Michael Rosen
& illustrated by Quentin Blake

'An infectiously funny bind-up'
Bookseller

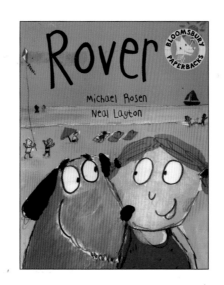

Rover

by Michael Rosen
& illustrated by Neal Layton

'A delight to behold'
Scotsman

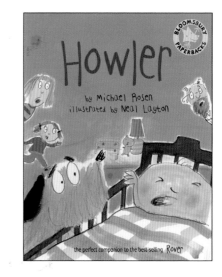

Howler

by Michael Rosen
& illustrated by Neal Layton

'A superb means of empathising
with a child who's a bit miffed
about a new arrival'
Observer